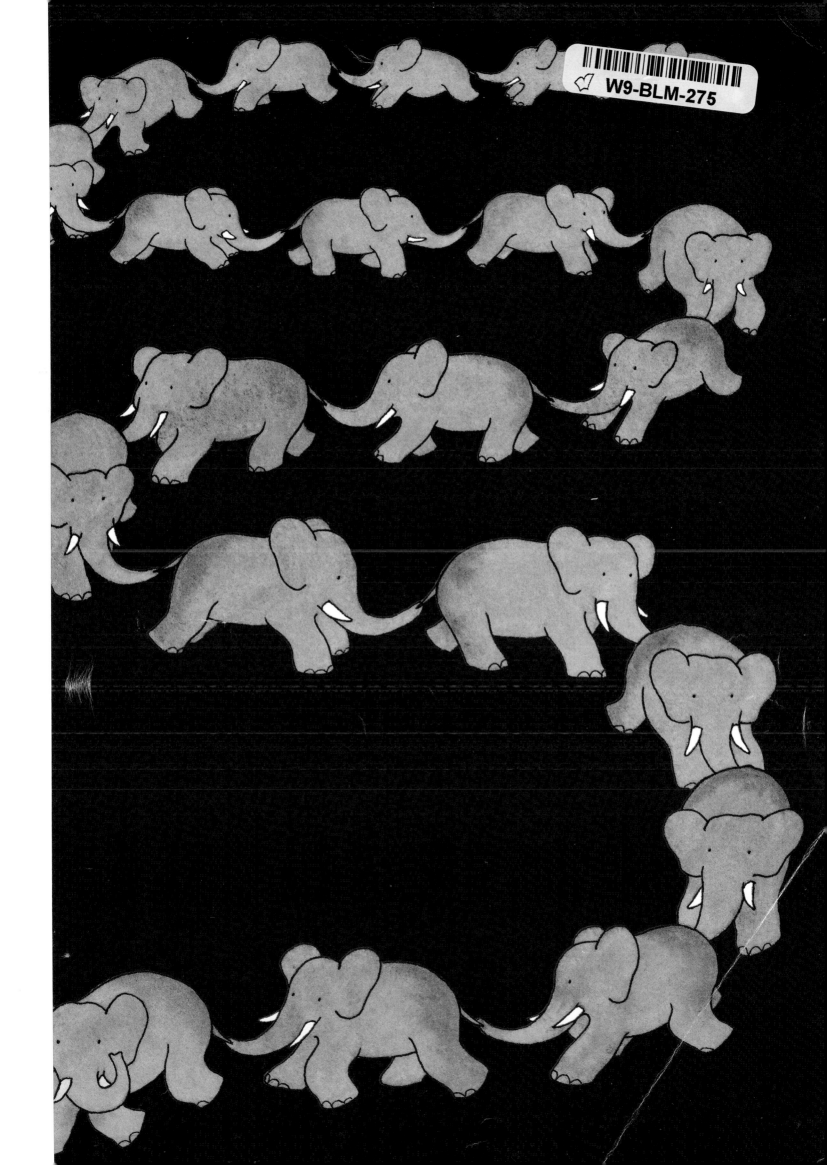

LAURENT DE BRUNHOFF

BABAR'S

Celesteville Games

Abrams Books for Young Readers

New York

The illustrations in this book were made with watercolor.

Cataloging-in-Publication Data has been applied for
and may be obtained from the Library of Congress.
ISBN 978-1-4197-0006-4

Text copyright © 2011 Phyllis Rose de Brunhoff
Illustrations copyright © 2011 Laurent de Brunhoff

Book design by Chad W. Beckerman

Printed and bound in China
10 9 8 7 6 5 4 3 2 1

Abrams Books for Young Readers are available at special discounts when
purchased in quantity for premiums and promotions as well as fundraising
or educational use. Special editions can also be created to specification. For
details, contact specialmarkets@abramsbooks.com or the address below.

THE ART OF BOOKS SINCE 1949

115 West 18th Street
New York, NY 10011
www.abramsbooks.com

Celesteville had become one of the world's
great cities and this year was hosting the
Worldwide Games. Athletes came
from all over to compete.

Babar's children, now grown up, went to see the warm-ups and practices. Pom and Isabelle liked swimming and diving best.

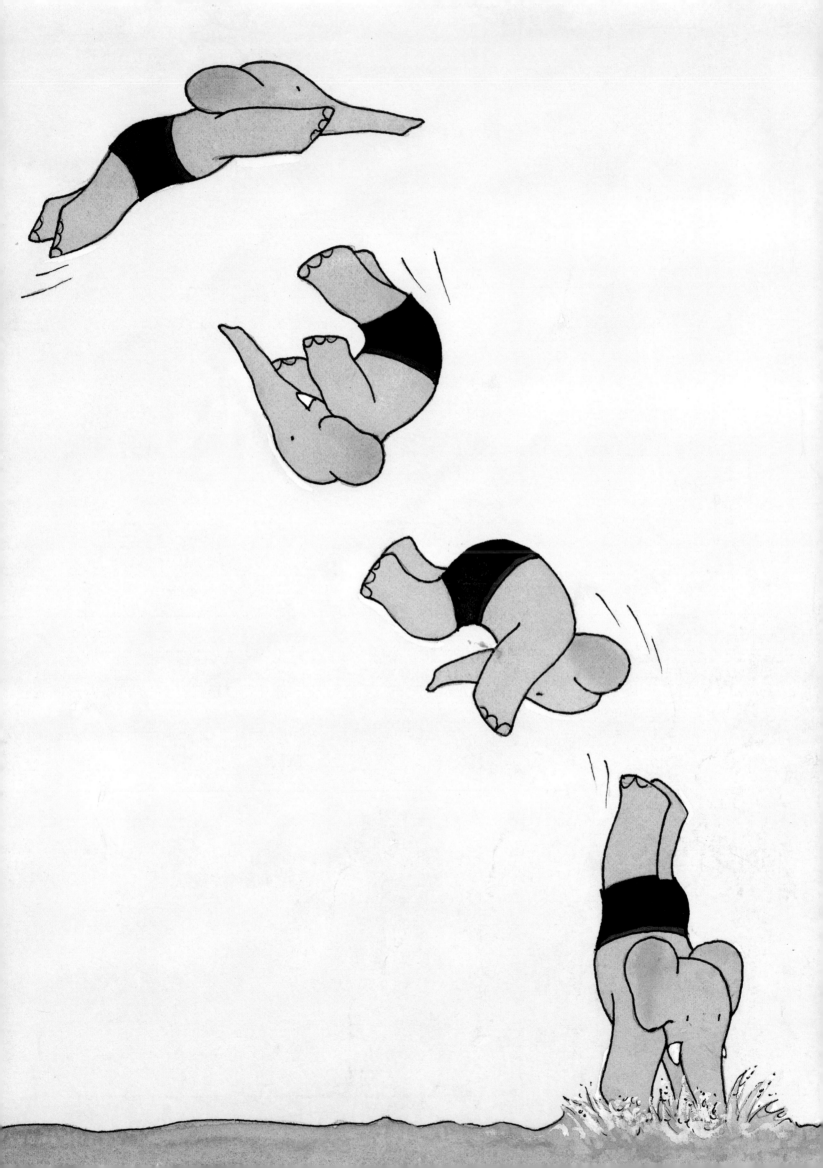

Flora and Alexander liked the track and field events.

And gymnastics!
Who would have thought that
hippos were almost as good at
the high bar as elephants?

Or that lions and tigers could be as graceful as they were strong and swift?

Flora especially liked to watch the pole vaulter from Mirza. She admired how he gathered his strength and then

Every day Flora went to his practices and one day even brought her mother, Celeste.

"Don't you think he's handsome?" Flora asked.

"Well," replied Celeste, "he is Mirzi, and the Mirzis have small ears."

"I think his ears are cute," said Flora firmly.

hurled himself into the air and over the bar.

That afternoon Flora was in the park. The pole vaulter walked up, texting, and sat beside her.

When he was finished, he noticed her and said, "It's you!"

"It's you!" replied Flora. "I've seen you jump."

"I've seen you in the stands."

"You saw me? With all those people?"

"You shine like a star," he said. "Will you tell me your name? Mine is Coriander—Cory for short."

"Coriander. That's a nice name. Mine is Flora."

"Flora! Beautiful as a flower, shining like a star!"

The Games opened officially that evening and the athletes paraded. When Cory passed Flora and her family, he dipped the Mirzi flag in salute.

"What a handsome boy," said Babar.

"Mom thinks his ears are too small," said Flora.

"Well," said Celeste, "he is Mirzi, and the Mirzis have small ears. But I am getting used to them, dear."

The next day Flora watched gymnastics, diving, and a bicycle race. But the thought of Cory wrapped itself around everything she saw. She couldn't wait to be with him again.

Cory, too, kept thinking about Flora. He said to himself, "I must do well for my country, but I also want to do well for Flora."

Whenever he could get away, Cory took Flora for walks in the park. They talked for hours about what they had done in the past and what they would do in the future.

"I want to be a doctor," said Cory.

"I want to be an artist," said Flora.

For Cory's main event, Flora was in the stands shouting, "Go Mirza! Go Mirza!" She waved a Mirzi flag. Many from Celesteville were surprised to see their princess backing another country's athlete.

"Is this OK?" Celeste asked Babar. "Should the princess of Celesteville cheer for another country?"

"I think it is love," said Babar. "And I think it will be good for all of us."

After the Games, Flora invited Cory for dinner with her family. She was so nervous that she made the cooks nervous, too. One of them dropped a chicken in the cake batter! Flora set the table with the knives on the left and the forks on the right.

"This is going to be a disaster," she cried.

"Don't be silly," her mother replied. "Remember, Cory will be as nervous as you. You must put him at ease."

Celeste was right. Cory's knees trembled as he stood at the front door. But as soon as he saw Flora, he felt fine.

Her brothers and sister welcomed him like a hero. "The athlete from the Games! Wow! I can't believe how high you jumped."

Soon he forgot that he'd been nervous at all. It was like being with his own family. The evening was a great success.

On Sunday Flora and Cory went for a picnic. After eating they lay on their backs looking at the sky.

"Check out that cloud, Flora," Cory said.

Flora looked where Cory was pointing. "It's skywriting!" she said.

As they watched, a little plane looped and dipped and spurted clouds that spelled out:

FLORA, MARRY ME.

Flora smiled and said, "Is that a question or an order?"

Cory replied, "It is an idea about our future which I hope you share."

"I do share it," Flora said. "And I will marry you."

The news of Flora's engagement spread quickly through Celesteville. Everyone was excited, especially Babar and Celeste. Zephir the monkey photographed Cory and Flora for the *Celesteville News*. Many others wanted pictures of the happy couple, too.

But Cory worried that his parents would not be happy to learn of his engagement. They had always wanted him to marry a girl from Mirza. Finally he video-called them and told them the news. He introduced them to Flora and her parents.

"It's true we wanted Coriander to marry a girl from Mirza," said his father. "But now that we meet you, Flora, how can we not love you? You are our princess in every way."

"However," added Cory's mother, "you would make us very happy if you had a Mirzi wedding."

"With pleasure!" said Flora.

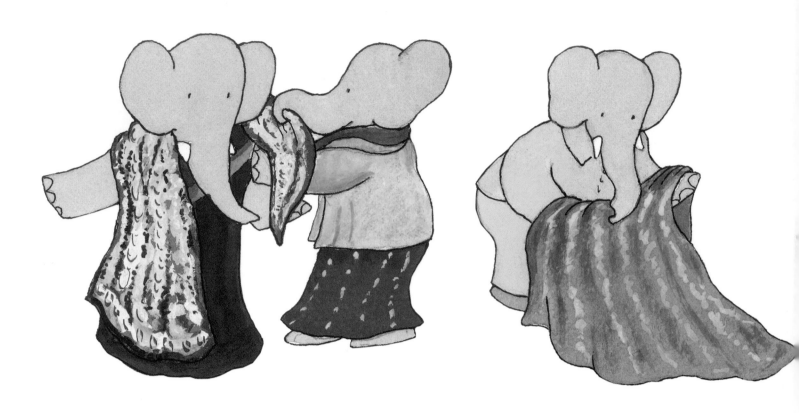

The people of Celesteville all tried to contribute to Flora's wedding. Some helped sew the Mirzi robes and dresses. Others prepared food or music. Still others picked flowers for garlands and gathered petals to throw in the air. Everyone was invited.

Many guests traveled from Mirza. Entertainers and helpers came from Mirza, too, some with magnificent Mirzi candelabras to light the way for the wedding procession.

Finally Cory's parents arrived and the festivities could begin! Cory rode in a chariot pulled by giraffes. His family, Flora's family, and many of their friends and guests danced around him as he was carried to his bride.

Flora waited for him on a stage, dressed in red, the color worn by Mirzi brides. Cory threw a garland of flowers over her head and she did the same to him. A blessing was said. They sat on the stage and the wedding guests came one by one to congratulate them. Flora and Cory sat there for hours, because everyone wanted to wish them well.

The birds of Celesteville had planned a surprise. At the end of the reception, an immense flock appeared, towing a giant basket in which the new couple would be flown to their honeymoon spot. After hugging their families good-bye, Flora and Cory climbed into the basket and were transported in style and comfort.

And Celesteville carried on.